A Cruel Fate

Also by Lindsey Davis

The Course of Honour
Rebels and Traitors
Master and God
Falco: The Official Companion

The Marcus Didius Falco Series
The Silver Pigs
Shadows in Bronze
Venus in Copper
The Iron Hand of Mars
Poseidon's Gold
Last Act in Palmyra
Time to Depart
A Dying Light in Corduba
Three Hands in the Fountain
Two for the Lions
One Virgin too Many
Ode to a Banker
A Body in the Bath House
The Jupiter Myth
The Accusers
Scandal Takes a Holiday
See Delphi and Die
Saturnalia
Alexandria
Nemesis

The Flavia Albia Series
The Ides of April
Enemies at Home (coming April 2014)

A Cruel Fate

Lindsey Davis

First published in Great Britain in 2014 by
Hodder & Stoughton
An Hachette UK company

1

Copyright © Lindsey Davis 2014

The right of Lindsey Davis to be identified as the
Author of the Work has been asserted by her in accordance
with the Copyright, Designs and Patents Act 1988.

All rights reserved. No part of this publication may be reproduced, stored in a retrieval system, or transmitted, in any form or by any means without the prior written permission of the publisher, nor be otherwise circulated in any form of binding or cover other than that in which it is published and without a similar condition being imposed on the subsequent purchaser.

All characters in this publication are fictitious and any resemblance to real persons, living or dead is purely coincidental.

A CIP catalogue record for this title is available
from the British Library

ISBN 978 1 444 76317 1

Typeset in Stone Serif by Palimpsest Book Production Ltd,
Falkirk, Stirlingshire

Printed and bound by CPI Group (UK) Ltd, Croydon, CR0 4YY

Hodder & Stoughton policy is to use papers that are natural, renewable and recyclable products and made from wood grown in sustainable forests. The logging and manufacturing processes are expected to conform to the environmental regulations of the country of origin.

Hodder & Stoughton Ltd
338 Euston Road
London NW1 3BH

www.hodder.co.uk

A Cruel Fate

Background

This story is set in the English Civil War, when King Charles I clashed with Parliament. They were at odds over money, religion and how the nation should be ruled. In the year 1642 this led to all-out war.

The King's soldiers were often called 'cavaliers' because the King had some fine troops of horsemen, or cavalry. Parliament's troops were mostly amateurs who had joined up to fight for political and religious freedoms. They were sometimes known as 'Roundheads' because some had been trade apprentices, who were made to wear short hair.

****

This story begins in December, four months after the war began. There has been one important battle, at Edgehill in the Midlands, which neither side really won. Now the armies are spending the winter trying to gain ground before the next year's fighting.

The King has fled from London and has made Oxford his base. Nearby towns that support Parliament are a real danger, so his soldiers will attack them. Places like Marlborough and Cirencester are in great danger. Most of the men who live in these country towns have never been soldiers, and they have no idea of what might happen when real fighting starts.

Chapter 1

The King Captures Marlborough

'Who burns books? What men are so wicked?'

As they loot the town, the King's soldiers make a bonfire in the street. They break into John Hammond's bookshop, then carry out armfuls of books, which they pile on the cobbles in rough heaps. They feed the bonfire with books for three hours. Martin Watts, who works for Hammond, watches them, amazed and helpless. He loses his doubts about the war, and decides which side he supports.

When he can no longer bear the sight of burning books, Martin tries to protest. A soldier strikes him over the head with a gun and knocks him down. Then he is taken prisoner. He is an unarmed member of the public. He cannot believe this is happening.

****

Martin is twenty-seven – a lean figure, neither

handsome nor ugly. He has always lived here in Wiltshire. He has little knowledge of war, but as he waits for the King's soldiers to deal with him, he understands that the attack was bound to happen. Marlborough is less than thirty miles from Oxford. The town strongly supports Parliament and has raised money and troops. The King cannot risk having enemies so close. Besides, in Marlborough there are many wealthy homes and a thriving market. The armies on both sides badly need funds. The King's soldiers have come to remove the danger posed by this rebel town, but also to look for booty and fun.

For days people have been afraid of what was coming. The river would protect them on the south side, but new earthworks were hastily built to guard the north. The moment they dreaded came on the eighth of December. After a dark night with stormy weather, four thousand of the King's soldiers (known as royalists) arrived. Their great cannon tried to pound the town, but the houses lay out of their range.

At first the royalists tried to make a grand show of their strength. They wanted to awe the town, in order to avoid a battle.

They captured a spy. Instead of hanging him, they paraded troops before him. Then they spared him. He was told to return home and warn people how large and gallant the King's army was – and how pointless it would be to resist.

The first real action was fitful, outside the town, as the royalists tried to break in to the town and the defenders fought to keep them out. Some royalists were killed in a short fight with muskets and pistols. Then a fiercer exchange of fire lasted for three hours, during which time not one defender fell. A barn full of the town's musketeers was set alight by a shell. Then a house behind it started to burn too. The rebels retreated. The royalists overtook them. Horsemen charged in at both ends of the town. Some royalists reached the main streets by bursting through a passage in one of the great inns. In triumph they cried out, 'A town! A town for King Charles!'

As long as they could, the rebels shot out of windows and defended barriers in the streets. Women helped to put out the fires, urging their husbands to keep fighting. But royalist foot-soldiers were soon clearing the barriers. Once the enemy were in the town, all discipline failed. The market traders, who had been given guns, threw them into the river and made a run for it. People were killed. There was noise, clouds of smoke, blood and bodies everywhere.

When the fighting ended, the King's men began to rob and destroy. They set more buildings on fire. They terrified people by invading their homes – slashing tables, breaking windows, stabling their horses in parlours. Property was stolen or simply wrecked. The happy royalists carried off barrels of oil, bottles of wine, vinegar, brandy, treacle, spices and dried fruit. One soldier set alight a shop filled with oil, hemp and tar. A neighbour put out the flames. Others tried to fire a draper's shop, but that blaze was quenched too. And they burned books. They wanted to shock. They wanted to terrorise.

****

Martin Watts surprised himself by making his protest about the books. And now he is forced to stand and wait, under guard, until the royalists have time to attend to their prisoners.

****

Face to face for the first time with the King's troops, Martin sees that some of them are half starved. No wonder they are so keen to take plunder. Many march without shoes or stockings. Others have no coats. People in the town who are wearing good clothes are made to exchange them with the soldiers. Those who think all cavaliers are rich noblemen in velvet cloaks are wrong. These ragged men are just hungry thieves – robbers let loose upon the people in the name of the King.

The royalists break into the town hall. Again, this pains Martin, a man who values documents. He watches in horror as they rummage through chests full of records, old charters and deeds, which they toss into the streets or carry off. At the same time, they load waggons with cheese and other goods to send to their base in Oxford. Fifty-three houses are burned down, together with seven barns full of corn that they cannot carry with them. The cavaliers steal goods to the value of £50,000 – an enormous sum – plus arms, ammunition and four cannon. They also take more prisoners.

Martin Watts watches as John Franklin, the town's Member of Parliament, is removed from his place with the others and dragged to a tree. Two of the King's commanders – Lord Digby and Lord Wilmott – threaten to hang the MP from the tree unless he tells them where his money is hidden. Martin does not see the end of this, but later Mr Franklin is back safe among the prisoners.

****

One hundred and twenty men, including Martin, are herded away. They leave their town behind, burned and smoking. Its people are stripped of all they own. Many are dead. It is a scene of misery. No one in quiet Marlborough has ever known such fear and grief.

On a dark, wintry night, the captives are driven on foot through fords and standing water. They are wet, cold and afraid. Before they set out to Oxford all of them are forced into one nasty, stinking stable. It already contains horses. One of the horses is dead.

Next morning, they wait in vain for food. Taken out of the stable, they are tied together in pairs by their arms. Then they are forced along like rogues and thieves, up to their knees in mud, along the badly kept road. A friend of Martin's sees this sad group passing. The royalists prevent him approaching. Another man who tries to speak to them is treated more cruelly – he is taken prisoner too and brought with them.

After a few miles, at a village called Lambourne, a kind man brings them food, but they are allowed no time to stop and eat it.

No one has had anything to drink. Martin has a violent thirst. When his comrades try to take up water from the road to sip, he sees them beaten in the face. The cavaliers will not even allow the men to pick up ice. As a child, Martin used to suck ice from puddles, learning to avoid the mud at the bottom of the piece. It was a game; he never thought he might do it out of desperation.

The journey takes four days. It is like this all the way.

Their numbers swell as the royalists pick up other captives. Men who are ploughing fields are taken, and men who look out from their houses simply to see the troops go by. Sometimes the King's men claim that these people are Roundheads, or that they are known to have fought at Marlborough. More often they do not bother with excuses. As the group travels, the royalists steal horses, fodder for horses, and food for themselves. They take away anything they like the look of. They cause havoc by stabling their horses in barns of good corn so that the grain is trampled on and spoiled.

****

By the time they reach Oxford, the prisoners are almost too weak to walk. Oxford is an army camp now, full of noise and packed with people. The colleges have been taken over by the King's court and his soldiers. Houses burst with extra tenants.

As the men from Marlborough stagger through the streets, soldiers, scholars and people of the town come out to watch. They shout insults. 'Roundheads! Rogues! Traitors!' Some even strike the helpless captives.

For the first time, Martin learns how it feels to be hated. It teaches him to hate in return. New times, new experiences. He has never been a soldier, he has never been abused. He has never suffered as he is about to suffer.

They enter the town at the West Gate. Oxford Castle looms over them. It is six hundred years old and stands beside a low man-made mound. The Keep is showing its age and a large crack runs down it, but the place hums with the noise of soldiers and prisoners, and is still formidable. In times of peace it has been used as the county courts and jail. Now it will be where the King locks up those who have defied him.

King Charles has put an officer in charge, a brute called William Smith. He is free to act as he likes, with no one to oversee him. He loves the power he holds. He uses it cruelly.

When they arrive at the castle, the Marlborough men are sent up a narrow, winding stair into Saint George's Tower.

Now their nightmare begins.

Chapter 2

The First Night

Martin is astonished by what happens at the castle. He argues with his captors, saying he is not a soldier, he has never been a soldier, this is all a mistake. They ignore him. He tries again, asking who is in charge. They laugh at him.

These guards are unfair and cruel in a way Martin Watts has never known before. He grew up in a gentle country town, and until now was an innocent.

When he is forced, with the other captives, up into the tower, he thinks it is another mistake. Surely the soldiers have failed to see there is no space for so many prisoners? Nearly two hundred of them are crammed in. They have shelter, but nothing more. Nothing at all. There is one room they can use, about six yards square. Those who cannot get in have to stay on the stairs. It is terribly cold. This is a hard winter and the old tower is freezing. A biting wind whistles in through the narrow slits from which arrows were fired at enemies in the years before guns.

Martin begins to fear that they will never have any food or water. Weak, famished and parched, he is afraid he will soon faint from thirst. Finally they are given a penny loaf each and a pot of beer. The beer is so bad, water would have been better.

He has managed to squeeze himself into the room. There is no fire, and no lights burn. They have to sleep on bare boards. Crammed in together with no space to move, men lie on top of each other. Slowly it dawns on Martin that this is how he will live for a long time – if he can survive.

Some men are so tired they fall asleep, with snores and grunts. Others moan, in pain from wounds. Will a surgeon be sent to tend them? Clearly not.

Unable to sleep, Martin lies awake filled with fear. He grows very quiet within himself. He does not know it, but he is in shock. He hears in his head the terrible noise of what happened at Marlborough. Wild images of his fallen town torment his mind.

He relives the siege. He sees again the piles of books being fed to the flames. He sees his own rage, remembers running to stop the cavaliers, dragging at a soldier's arm in protest. He is clubbed with a gun. He falls to the ground, which may have saved his life. Now he is at the castle, his cold fingers can feel dried blood on his scalp and a great bump. He knows it could have been worse. Two hundred people were killed in Marlborough that day. Most of them were people he knew.

Martin loves books. He owns none, for he is a poor man, but he has read them in the bookshop. Never again. When the King's men destroyed Hammond's stock and burned his shop, the shop where Martin worked, they stole Martin's livelihood. Only now does this properly dawn on him.

What is to happen to him now?

One change has started. Already Martin Watts is growing harder than he was before the siege. While the civil war was brewing over the past few years, he was reading news-sheets that were sold in the shop. These told him why Parliament is at war with the King. Martin has followed the reasons and believes open rebellion had to happen. He hates unjust acts and unfair taxes. He wants his rights, the freedom to make of his life whatever he can. He wants liberty to think what he chooses – the right to worship God in his own way. When those harsh guards pushed him into this freezing tower, they made sure that if he ever leaves, he will be one more rebel against them.

Some of the men with him in the tower are thinking of their families, but Martin has no one. His brothers and sisters died young; his parents are dead now too. As he shivers in Oxford Castle, he has never felt so alone in the world.

He is not married. Knowing he cannot afford a wife, he has kept to himself and no young woman has caught his eye. But this means he has nobody outside who will miss him. No one will want to find out where he has been locked up. No one will try to get him out. No one will pay a ransom for him.

Here he is. Here he must stay. One penny loaf and a pot of beer – on the days when the guards provide it. Otherwise, nothing.

Chapter 3

The Provost Marshal

The man in charge of the prison is called William Smith. His rank is captain. So he is a junior officer of the King's – junior, and yet he holds great power. Too much power.

He has another title, Provost Marshal. In an army, the Provost Marshal has the special duty of keeping order among the soldiers. Snug in the castle, Smith does not concern himself with that duty.

From time to time, the rules of war are read out to the army. It has even been known for the King to have soldiers hanged for stealing from the public – to show that His Majesty respects the rules of war. On the whole, though, discipline is not prized in the King's army.

At the King's prison in Oxford, conditions are more grim than most. But Martin Watts does not know that. He has led a quiet life and never committed any crime. He has no idea what life is like when people are locked up. He will learn quickly.

At this time a jailer is required to supply only the most basic things to keep his prisoners alive. It is said that the King allows sixpence a day per man, and maybe King Charles believes he does. But Smith only spends one penny farthing – a penny loaf of bread and one drink of weak beer each. In all jails prisoners have to pay extra for anything else. Laundry, better food, a fire . . . in bad prisons you must even pay for a place *near* the fire. Smith does not allow any of that. He gives captured officers slightly better treatment than the ordinary soldiers, but even officers are not allowed to buy comforts.

The men from Marlborough begin to hear things about William Smith. They do not like what they hear. All too soon, they see for themselves.

One loaf a day is all they have to eat for many weeks. Some go two days at a time with no food at all. They still have only bare floorboards to lie on. A little straw is laid down, but that is where they must piss and shit. There are no latrines or chamber pots. The filth is so deep it comes over their shoes.

They all grow very weak. Many fall sick. There is a great risk that jail fever will kill them – the feared 'bloody flux', which is probably typhus. One man starves to death. As he draws towards his end, others appeal to Smith to allow some help. The officers beg him to ease the invalid's distress. He refuses and the man dies.

He is just the first.

****

A few days later Smith has the men taken down to the castle yard. He makes them stand there while he reads out an oath he wants them all to sign. He asks them to swear they will change sides and support the King. The prisoners refuse. It is against their beliefs. They bravely reply that they have already sworn to support 'King and Parliament' – which is the rebels' way of claiming that they are loyal to proper government.

At that, Smith flies into a huge rage. Martin Watts wonders if the King has ordered Smith to force the prisoners to submit. The angry jailer calls them damned rogues and traitors. He beats them with a stick as he drives them back up into the tower.

Now his rule becomes even harsher. He has permitted no one to bring them food or clean shirts, but he discovers a hole in the wall, through which things have been delivered by well-wishers. He has the hole blocked up, and forbids people on pain of death to bring anything else.

If friends send any food into the castle for the prisoners, his soldiers steal and eat it.

So great is the men's misery that the officers and gentlemen who are imprisoned with them, and who have money, decide to donate a weekly sum of money. The collection is intended to buy bread and beer for the poorer men. Without this act of charity, half the men would be dead. Smith hears what is going on, so he stops it and threatens death to the steward who had been put in charge of the cash.

A short time later, one of the King's generals, Sir James Pennimen, needs more soldiers. Once again the Marlborough men are taken down to the castle yard. On their way, they pass a room where some gentlemen have washed at a basin. Parched prisoners rush to this basin and cannot be restrained from drinking the dirty slops. Down in the castle yard, they defy the jailers again as they lap standing rainwater from the tops of barrels.

The royalists go through the same process as before. They demand that the captives change sides and fight for the King. Again the prisoners refuse. Pennimen curses them. He threatens to withhold food from them entirely, saying, 'Those who will not work, shall not eat.' Smith joins in with angry oaths, then chases them back up the tower, beating them with his stick.

Smith decides the prisoners will stay on their cruel tiny food allowance. He tells them, 'I will make you shit as small as rats!'

****

Smith never stops his efforts to persuade them to change sides. The man is so desperate to win them round, that it seems as if he will be in trouble if he fails.

He tries again. He calls them back and lines them up in the yard. As he argues the case for them to change sides, he even quotes from the Bible. According to Smith, none of them will find salvation unless they join the King's army.

They still refuse. He rages. Knowing now what he is like, they wait in dread to see how he will punish them.

****

Monday the sixth of February is a black day. Smith takes forty of the prisoners away from the castle. Martin has the bad luck to be one of them.

Smith sends them to an even worse prison, a local lock-up called Bridewell. To Martin's horror, they are put underground in a dungeon.

There is so little room they cannot move or even sit. The fetid place is filthy and stinks. There is nowhere for them to piss or shit, so each man has to do that where he stands. The floor does not drain. Soon they are standing up to their ankles in their own piss and shit.

Captain Smith keeps them there for the next four weeks. That is, he keeps those who survive.

****

As he tries to bear this misery, Martin prays to the Lord. He thinks bitterly about the monster, Smith. Given power, Provost Marshal Smith uses it with no restraint. Why should he? He behaves like this because nobody stops him. He calls it the fortune of war. The more he gets away with cruelty, the more he believes he has the King's consent. He convinces himself that this is what his royal master wants. Maybe that is true.

Either way, Smith has no fear of god or man. He has no conscience. Martin Watts begins to see the King in the same way. King Charles, too, views his subjects as less than human – he believes God gave him the right to rule, and he can do so in whatever way he chooses.

Chapter 4

Cirencester Falls Too

In February, another rebel town is in trouble.

Armies try not to fight in winter. There is a reason for that. When Nat Afton is captured by the King's men at Cirencester, he starts to find out why.

****

To King Charles, Cirencester is important because it lies on the way to the rebel centre at Gloucester, which he wants to capture. Cirencester is rich – a wool town, with many merchants trading in cloth.

The town committed to Parliament's side early in the conflict – last August. At that time a lively scene took place when a royalist, Lord Chandos, tried to raise troops for the King. The ordinary people were against King Charles and his high-handed style of ruling, although the gentry and clergymen remained loyal to him.

Lord Chandos met a hostile reception. People urged him to promise to uphold the freedom of Parliament. Chandos tried not to commit himself. A rowdy mob gathered, and Chandos became so nervous that he departed without fuss. He left his coach behind in the town centre, as a decoy. The coach was torn apart in protest the next day.

Nat Afton helped to wreck the coach. He enjoyed it so much, he joined up to fight as a rebel. Always a little feckless, he cared nothing for politics, but he hoped to get a uniform, new shoes and free rations.

****

A few months later, Nat starts to regret this. True, he has a warm coat, bread and cheese and beer every day, and a knapsack to hold the Bible they have given him (though he has sold the Bible secretly). In January he feels concerned when Prince Rupert, King Charles's glamorous German nephew, appears near the town with his soldiers. Rupert is clearly planning an attack. Nat has no wish to fight. He thinks about running away, but is too lazy to do anything about it. In any case, the Prince then leaves.

But Prince Rupert comes back in February,

with about six thousand troops – a small army. Nat feels nervous, but he finds himself caught up in the excitement. He sees cannon set up and extra soldiers brought in. He wonders what fighting will be like. When he says this to his sister Jane, she tells him straight that it might be better not to find out.

Jane is the sensible one in their family.

****

Before the royalist troops can enter the town, they have to capture the heavily defended Barton Mill. First they cause confusion by setting fire to barns, haystacks and houses. The rebels try to fend them off, firing their two cannon. But the royalists break through a barrier of wood, carts and chains that has been set up at the bottom of a hill. Then Prince Rupert and his cavalry thunder into the town, following the line of Black Jack Street into the marketplace.

The cavaliers shoot with pistols at any rebels they see, as they make a clear path for their foot-soldiers to follow. In return, shots are fired at the royalists from houses. A tailor who is holding the rebels' banner is shot dead by a sniper. Three hundred other defenders are killed. Both Barton Mill and the Spitalgate have been overrun. More and more royalist troops now stream through the streets, while the rebels flee over the water meadows and river.

The assault takes an hour and a half. Afterwards there is serious looting and all houses belonging to those who resisted the Prince – and even some belonging to royalists – are burned. The victors seize over a thousand prisoners, including two puritan ministers. They take them to a field to be reviewed by the royalist commanders. The prisoners are stripped of their shoes and stockings, hats and doublets. Gentlemen have their britches stolen. All shivering, and some of them wounded too, they are locked in the parish church overnight. Nat is one of them.

The prisoners are marched off the next day. Like the men from Marlborough, they have a horrible, bitter-cold journey. At least a small piece of cheese is given to each of them before they start. For two days they are driven along, tied together with match cord. At Burford they receive a piece of bread each, but only after they have waited for hours on a hill in freezing weather. Most are barefoot and with bare legs. An icy wind howls around them and they are standing in snow.

At Witney they stay overnight in another church. Finally they come to Oxford. The King himself rides out to view them, bringing his two young sons, the Prince of Wales and the Duke of York. So these two beautifully dressed young boys are taught to jeer at distressed subjects, watching them being driven along like dogs or horses, not men.

Nat Afton sees now why a war against the King is being fought.

****

Held in Oxford Castle, the new prisoners from Cirencester are taken out daily to help build great earth walls around Oxford to protect the city and the King.

Within a month Cirencester humbly submits to the King, and apologises for rebelling. The town and the gentry from surrounding areas are fined the huge sum of £4,000 a month, plus £3,000 straight away to pay for the upkeep of the King's garrison. Cirencester is given a royalist governor.

After the town apologises, most of its prisoners are freed and allowed to go home. Over a thousand of the captured rebels have now taken the oath to support the King. But sixteen men have refused.

Nat Afton is one who refuses. He is one of the men who do not return home.

Chapter 5

Jane Has to Look for Her Brother

Nat Afton has three sisters. Two of them, Mary and Lucy, are married with children. Mary is due to give birth to another baby any day. When Nat fails to arrive home with the other men, Mary and Lucy put their heads together. They inform the third sister that they have enough to do. So, it must be Jane's task to find out where their brother is.

Jane Afton is a spinster in both senses of that word: she is a single woman and she spins wool for a living. The cloth merchants around Cirencester use home-workers to prepare their thread. Jane and her sisters do this – but Jane has the bad luck to be a spinster in the other sense too. Since she is now twenty-three, in the eyes of the world Jane is an old maid. Only when she feels very low in spirits does she think ruefully that she has stayed single because she is the sensible one.

All the Afton girls work hard, because they

are poor people and they have to. When they go to church on Sundays, they hope the parson will speak loudly in his sermon. If not, they risk falling asleep from weariness. For the two wives, having a second income takes the pinch out of very tight home budgets. With what she earns, Jane is able to rent a tiny cottage. One up, one down. Smaller than many stables.

Jane would rather live alone than be a burden on one of her sisters – which, everyone knows, means they will make her a household drudge. But soon she will have to face that because, if she keeps living alone, people will think she is not just an old maid but an old witch. That would be too dangerous.

Like her sisters, Jane is a shrewd, neat woman with a country complexion and a town wit. She can tell beans from peas. She is strong enough to scrub a pot clean even after a stew has stuck in it. She is a determined woman who will bother to do that.

Her steadiness will be vital when she tries to find out what has happened to Nat.

****

Like many brothers, at all times in history, Nat is not quite the brother a sister would choose.

Still not twenty, he is a light lad. He had a trade once. It only lasted seven months. He worked for a dyer and could have become a dyer himself, if he had tried. He *thought* he had tried. The dyer thought differently. It all went wrong, although Nat assured his sisters it was not his fault. They knew him, so they knew better.

For Nat to have volunteered as a soldier was no real surprise. This was just one in a series of jobs he drifts in and out of. Jane had expected him to tire of it. She thought Nat would prefer to wander through life, spending times with a beer tankard in one tavern or another. He is not a hard drinker. He just likes to take life easy. If ever he is in trouble, he knows one of his sisters will see him through it. Mary and Lucy's husbands may grumble and forbid them to help, but Nat will move on to the next sister. He can always rely on Jane.

Well, Jane is a spinster, an old maid. What else does she have to do, but look out for her feckless brother? Nat, who has sweet honest charm, even used to point this out when he came to cadge off her.

****

As a soldier, Nat is half-hearted. He has no idea

of the politics in this civil war. Oliver Cromwell, the most famous rebel general, will draw a bleak contrast between the troops on the two sides, saying: *'I had rather have a plain, russet-coated captain that knows what he fights for and loves what he knows, than that which you call a gentleman and is nothing else.'*

Men of humble birth may sometimes become officers, but Nat Afton will never be a captain. He will not aspire to it. He wants to lie low. It is a great surprise to Jane that he has even been taken prisoner. In her heart, she knows it was more like Nat to run away when Prince Rupert's soldiers attacked.

Yet in a way Nat fits Oliver Cromwell's description. Cromwell will also admit that not all rebel soldiers are good, worthy men. *'Your troopers are most of them old decayed servingmen and tapsters,'* he says of his own side, while of the King's, *'their troopers are gentlemen's sons, younger sons and persons of quality . . .'*

This could be said of Nat. He really is a tapster, a man who turns the beer tap in a pub. If landlords give him a few pence for it, he serves beer and ale from the barrel in the taverns where he drinks. He is not 'decayed' as Cromwell calls it, not old, lame and toothless – but that will come. Even Jane, who loves him although she can see his faults, knows what will happen. Nat will go downhill at an early age.

The right wife could stop it and save him, say their sisters Mary and Lucy. This is wishful thinking. Jane, being the sensible one, thinks that living with Nat would be too hard on a woman. But she keeps this to herself. Spinsters are not allowed to have opinions on married life.

Nat Afton has caused his sisters worry since he was a child, and Jane has borne most of the burden. So now she accepts quietly that she must go to Oxford, looking for him. She has never been out of her home county before. Her sisters show their support by finding the money to pay a carrier to take her. Families must rally round.

Jane has no idea what she has taken on.

Chapter 6

Jane Reaches Oxford

When Jane Afton arrives at Oxford, she begins to learn what war means. She is shocked. She does not expect people to be stopped from going into the town. But this is now the King's capital city. He has made it safe from attack, and work is still in hand. A Dutch engineer, an expert who knows about sieges, is here to oversee that. Ordinary life has changed.

Huge earth walls, patrolled by guards, circle the city. Watchtowers look over all the countryside around. Bridges are barred. Even the River Thames is blocked with booms that have been laid across the water. Some of the walls were built by students. People of the town are supposed to help, though they often refuse to turn up and are fined. After the Cirencester prisoners were pardoned and returned home, Jane heard from them how they were forced to take up picks and shovels to do this hard labour. Maybe Nat took part. He would not like that.

Sentries question anyone who wants to enter Oxford. Entering through the military lines is the first task Jane faces. You need a pass, and she does not have one. To issue a pass, the King's soldiers have to know you. Even then, they must like your reason for coming. Asking about a prisoner of war will mark you as one of the enemy. Jane sees at once that it is better not to ask. Better not to make them notice her.

She starts to use her wits. Food is needed here in great quantities. Anyone supplying food gets special treatment. In the end, Jane makes friends with an old woman from a farm who brings butter to sell, and slips past the guards with her.

****

The high Mound, with the broken-down old Keep alongside, makes the castle easy to find. She makes her way to Saint George's Tower, which is also easy to see. Jane looks up in fear at this square, grey, stone building, which was built to scare away enemies with its size and strength. Is her brother somewhere high up inside? If so, what pitiful state has he been reduced to? The Cirencester men brought home grim stories of Marshal Smith's cruelty. Already nervous, Jane hurries to ask about her brother.

Now she runs into an unexpected setback.

Jane has presumed that the soldiers will at least tell her if Nat is being kept here. Maybe they will let her see him. She wants to take in warm food and a clean shirt. Why not?

What happens shocks her. The harsh men on guard laugh at her requests. They say they do not know if Nat is there. It is all new to Jane, but she soon sees that they turn away the friends of their unhappy prisoners every day. The soldiers seem to enjoy rejecting applicants. Still, something about Jane Afton is winning. She is a dainty young woman, with steady brown eyes and a polite air. She does not curse the soldiers or insult them – not yet. She asks very quietly if they will explain, so she can understand.

Bored, one soldier tells her the rules, rules that he loves applying. He savours Jane's disappointment. No one can go in. Even the wives of officers are kept out. No one can send in anything to help the prisoners.

Foolishly, Jane asks if she can speak to the person in charge.

When the soldier stops yelling with laughter, he describes the Provost Marshal and gives horrible details of how Smith treats his prisoners. In case Jane hopes she can ransom her brother, the soldier warns her off. 'Do you have ten pounds?'

'No, sir.' Jane has never seen so much money. 'But I will try to see what I can find . . .'

'We had a Mr Edward Bradney here. He thought payment for his freedom had been agreed. But he offered Marshal Smith only four pounds, when he knew the price was ten.'

'And what happened?'

'Our Marshal snatched the four, and sent Mr Bradney back to prison. He escaped, but we easily took him again.' Jane wonders if Nat could have escaped – but if so, why has he not come home? 'No one escapes us,' sneers the soldier. 'Bradney has been here six more months. Now he is dying in his own piss and filth. That will teach him to rebel against the King.'

Shaking and upset, Jane tries mentioning Cirencester, and how the town has apologised to the King.

The soldier knows all about it. 'Oh such a humble apology! All meekly done, to avoid your filthy town losing everything. "*They admit that their own errors exposed them to the anger of His Majesty's justly enraged army.*" Well, His Majesty has shown them mercy and so the cowards have all crept home in shame.'

'Not all. Not my brother. I do not understand why.'

'He is a rebel and a traitor. He must have

refused to swear the oath of loyalty to His Majesty.'

Jane knows that over a thousand men from Cirencester did sign that oath. She cannot imagine Nat taking a stand against it, not when so many caved in. He follows the crowd, to keep out of trouble. Nat would want to be safe back home as soon as possible; he must want to be sitting in a warm tavern, getting a free pot of ale for entertaining the landlord with his adventures.

'That would be a mistake,' Jane falters. 'He cannot have meant it.'

'I don't think so!' jeers the guard. 'A man must answer for himself.' A new thought strikes him. 'Or here's another reason, maid – your brother has died!'

'If that were so, somebody would know, surely?'

As Jane falters, the heartless soldier sneers. 'Who can say? We keep no count. The dead are left to rot up there among the living.'

At first Jane assumes he has invented this to scare her – then she grasps the truth. He means it.

Blinded by tears, she stumbles away.

Chapter 7

Jane Learns More

It was early morning when Jane came into Oxford with the farmer's wife who sells butter. After her grim visit to the castle, she spends most of the day wandering about. What can she do now? Must she go home empty-handed, without even news?

Her two sisters have convinced themselves that Jane will find Nat and bring him back home with her. Having no idea of the truth, they expect this to happen quickly. Jane always had doubts. Now she feels the heavy burden of her new knowledge. The civil war will not be over soon. The huge earth walls she has seen around Oxford warn her that the country is in the midst of a great conflict.

Already it is six months since the King raised his flag and began to gather an army. Jane realises that the war has hardly begun. People will have to live with it for years. Life in quiet English towns like Cirencester will cease to be normal. Children will grow up never knowing peace.

And people will suffer. Young men like Nat, who thought they would lead simple lives, will find that all is changed. Many will suffer in ways they had never expected. Many will die – not from the usual causes of disease and poverty, but directly because of this war.

Jane thinks about her talk with the soldier earlier. The way the man spoke, it sounded as if it is a common event for a prisoner to die at the castle. Maybe – she makes herself face this terrible possibility – maybe her brother really is one of the dead.

****

The streets are packed with people. Many take no notice of Jane Afton. However, some of the men, the soldiers, eye her up. She starts to feel unsafe. She is carrying a bundle – a few things for herself and old clothes that the family put together for Nat. This luggage marks her out as a woman alone in a strange town – a woman who can be preyed upon.

She has nowhere to stay. The butter woman has warned her that houses here are crammed with too many people. There is no room for anybody new. Jane begins to feel anxious for herself.

In the afternoon, she treks back to the castle. The guards have changed, but their story stays the same. Pleading for news is hopeless. This time other people are there, people with the same request as hers. Among them are male friends of the prisoners, but most are women – wives trying to see their husbands. They all look strained. As they plead for access and are refused, Jane can tell that this hideous ritual happens every day. Over and over again, Marshal Smith is mentioned by the guards as the reason for their cruelty. Everyone seems afraid of him, even his own men.

As she waits her turn to be rebuffed, Jane takes more notice of the royalist soldiers. They are rough men, who lounge about and smoke clay pipes even while they are on duty. They wear poor clothes, but have guns and swords. Their manners are as crude as their task. And their task is simple: to make prisoners suffer, and even to demoralise the prisoners' friends.

In war, as Jane starts to understand, armies want to reduce their enemy's numbers. If it does not happen in battle, they will let it happen through neglect. That may be the easiest way. And taking away hope is a useful way to lessen any enemy's will to continue.

As she listens and watches, she overhears a conversation. On the stairs that lead up into the tower, a man who must be one of the prisoners hoarsely pleads with a soldier for water. He sounds desperate. Still the reply comes that Smith has forbidden it. The soldier dare not give him a drink – 'Not even though the river runs right at our door.'

Jane is sure she hears the sound of someone being beaten. She is relieved when a door slams shut, cutting off the noise.

One of the louts on guard sees his chance with Jane. He makes an attempt to put his arms around her. She cannot defend herself, except by breaking free of him and running from the guardhouse.

In tears, Jane bumps into a woman just outside. She is the wife of one of the officers who are being held. She is called Mrs Wingate. Seeing Jane's distress, she takes pity and brings Jane back to her own lodgings. Although there are no beds free anywhere in that house, she says Jane can stay today. She may sleep on the tall wooden settle, by the fire in the kitchen – provided they can hide this from the landlord. So, for one night, Jane Afton will be safely off the streets.

****

That evening, Mrs Wingate provides a plain meal for them both and, as they eat it, she explains what Jane is dealing with.

'Marshal Smith is killing them with his cruelty. He keeps even the captains and gentlemen locked up day and night, with sentries always on guard. Smith allows them no contact with the living or the dead, with men or books. He denies them pen, ink and paper to write to their friends for relief. They pine for bread and water. They cannot walk in the fresh air.'

'Have you managed any contact?' Jane asks, thinking that the wife of an officer surely must have better treatment. But her companion shakes her head.

Mrs Wingate is a well-spoken woman, with a little education. She has left her pantry and herb garden, her wash-copper and bread oven, even her small children, to come to Oxford and do what she can for her man. In her, Jane sees how women must now step out of the role normally given to them. Wives of prisoners have to take charge of their families in ways they never expected. It falls to them to try to help their men, to struggle to arrange a ransom or a prisoner exchange. Alone, they have to keep their families together. All the time, they know their men may never come home again.

Mrs Wingate tells what she knows about William Smith, the bully who holds such extreme power over the prisoners.

'This is a degenerate and bloody fellow, Jane. He turned himself from being a mere cobbler to a position at the royal court. He was supposed to keep order among those who attended the royal court and to act as a bailiff. But Smith lost his place for bad behaviour. Then he took up as a go-between for thieves, pick-pockets and every kind of rogue. To this day, he keeps company with such villains. The worst thing about him is that he was arrested for having two wives. He could have been hanged for that. Indeed, he should have been!'

Jane is shocked. 'And why is such a wicked man put in this position? Why does the King trust him?'

She observes how Mrs Wingate purses her lips. The two women sit in silence for a moment. Women are not supposed to engage in politics, nor even to hold opinions, but King Charles has hardened these two women's attitudes. The King's appointment of Smith may be mere lack of judgement – or a much worse decision on his part. The women know what they think.

Chapter 8

Worse News for Jane

Next day, Captain Wingate's wife takes Jane with her for the rite of begging to see the prisoners. Now that Jane is braced for bad news, Mrs Wingate tells her more about how the men in jail are treated.

'You must be prepared, my dear. They are starved, beaten, and many of them are chained up. There is a cruel way of doing that. The soldiers call it "neck and heels" – they are trussed up in iron chains like poultry, and unable to move. Sometimes as much as thirty-five pounds' weight of metal is loaded on them. You cannot imagine their pain.'

'And they must be weakened anyway by lack of food and drink.' Jane describes how she heard a prisoner pleading for water.

'I have heard some there are so thirsty they have drunk their own urine,' Mrs Wingate tells her angrily. 'Decent folk would not believe what is done to them. Once, when prisoners were fainting for lack of water, Smith took the keys from a guard who was about to give them some. He put his own man in chains for that, then later stripped him of his clothes and turned him out of doors.'

'So his soldiers are taught never to show pity?' Jane whispers.

'His men have learned to be brutes from his example. He has a deputy, a man called Roche, who is as bad as him. Roche does sell beer to the prisoners, and then charges great prices, but mostly the guards take joy in refusing even water.'

'But the prisoners will die!' cries Jane, who is still very innocent. 'Or is that the intention?'

'I believe it is,' confirms Mrs Wingate grimly. 'With such abuse comes plague. Many of the men inside the tower are very sick. In that condition, they are forced to lie on bare boards, on or under tables, in the hearths, on the stairs, or even upon each other.'

'No wonder they die.'

'Indeed, Jane. Fever comes from being so close to sickness. Infection is also spread by their sad corpses – for Smith makes no arrangements to remove dead bodies or provide proper funerals. The prisoners are compelled to find money among themselves if they want the dead men removed.'

Jane cannot avoid the dreadful thought that Nat may have been one of those corpses – carried off by plague and buried only through the kindness of his companions.

With a lump in her throat again, Jane lets slip her fears that her search is hopeless. Mrs Wingate tries to cheer her. She points out a woman, heavily pregnant, who she says is Elizabeth Lilburne. She is a merchant's daughter who last year married a well-known opponent of the King's policies. Captain John Lilburne was in a rebel garrison at Brentford near London when King Charles's men attacked the city. As the cavaliers approached, Lilburne tried to escape by jumping into the Thames, but was captured and brought to Oxford. At that time he was the most prominent opponent they had taken, so they planned to try him for high treason – which carried a sentence of death.

Lilburne already knew all about the harsh treatment the authorities gave anyone who defied the King. Arrested in the past for publishing unlawful writings, he had once been flogged with a three-thonged whip on his bare back. With his hands tied to the rear of a cart, he was dragged from prison to the pillory. Even when stooping in the stocks, he managed to campaign for freedom, until in the end he was gagged. Finally he was thrown back in prison, but even there he managed to write. He printed an account of his own punishment, which he called *The Work of the Beast*.

Now he is suffering in Oxford jail.

'If they bring him to trial, Jane, they will hang him without mercy. So his wife has shown what a woman of spirit can and must do. She took herself to Parliament. Captain Lilburne is not popular there, because he holds extreme views. But Elizabeth brought a petition and insisted it be heard.'

'So did Parliament respond?' asks Jane, enthralled.

'Yes, because if Lilburne were hanged, it would set a fatal precedent for all other prisoners. With only two days before the planned trial, Elizabeth – who is, as you see, carrying their first child – somehow raced back to Oxford and slipped through the lines.' Jane raises her eyebrows, knowing how difficult that is. 'Parliament declared that if Captain Lilburne, or any of his comrades, is killed, then an equal number of royalists will be put to death.'

'And has it worked?'

'Indeed. The trial was halted. John Lilburne now waits for an exchange of prisoners. Elizabeth stays here for his release.'

****

Because Captain Wingate's wife has been in Oxford for many weeks, she has made contacts. She is able to find Jane a room to stay in, a poor place that Jane must share, but it is better than no place at all. Jane still wants to believe she will not have to remain in Oxford for long. She takes the offer. She has brought a little money, her savings.

Her hopes of a short stay soon seem foolish. But she will not wilt helplessly when fate seems against her. So Jane begins a determined search for information. All it brings is worse news of Marshal Smith's degrading treatment of his charges.

From her poor lodgings in a tiny cottage in the backstreets, Jane learns where to find the women who once earned a few pence by helping prisoners. These thin, sad creatures are themselves close to starving. But in the past they took food and clean linen to men in trouble at the castle, also at the other prison called Bridewell, and in parish churches where the cavaliers hold many captives.

Smith has prevented the poor women's work. They themselves are suffering now, having lost the tiny income upon which they once relied.

They tell Jane that the prisoners are filthy and afflicted with lice, as well as starving and ill. Of those that have been beaten, some were hit with such force they have lost limbs.

****

Thinking that her brother may be ill, Jane sets out to learn what happens to the sick. She hears of a surgeon whom Marshal Smith engaged at one time for the men from Marlborough. Jane is not afraid of asking, so she tracks down where the man lives.

His name is Mr Betterise. At first he seems wary of talking to her, but he quickly becomes indignant at how Smith treated him.

'He gave me five shillings at the start.' This is no small sum. Jane wants to feel encouraged that money was provided – though she fears she will hear worse news. She is right. Mr Betterise cannot give her good cheer. 'I was to bring warm food and dress their wounds. I spent two shillings, which I gave to those poor women who used to feed the prisoners in the churches. But one day I ran into that monster in the street.'

'Marshal Smith?' Jane feels her heart sink. 'What did he do? I know he is unreasonable.'

'He is vile and dishonest.'

'Tell me the worst, sir, please.'

'When he saw me in the street, suddenly his mind changed. He demanded that I give him his money back. Even though I had spent some, he wanted the full five shillings.'

'So you could not help the poor wounded men?'

'Worse than that. I made the mistake of complaining to my neighbours of how Smith mistreats the men, how he denies them water. Smith heard of it. He came for me and threw me too into prison. I was lucky. Sir Jacob Astley, the King's commander, ordered me to be set free – but after that Smith would never let me in to attend to the wounded.'

His face clouds. He tells Jane sad stories he has heard. Two men who escaped were recaptured; Smith had their hands burned to the bone between their fingers. No surgeon was allowed to help them. Then they were each loaded with twenty-eight pounds of iron chains until they ended their days in torment. A captive brought in from Banbury had been wounded in the head with a poleaxe – a vicious cavalry weapon. The captains and gentlemen begged for medical help, but it was refused and the man died.

'I heard of men beaten with canes, maybe

sixty times, beaten on the head until the blood ran down over their ears. Men made to stand on the cold stone of the castle yard for three or four days and nights, in bitter winter. It is said men are dying in the foul dungeon at Bridewell – as many as two or three every day. There is no way I can help these poor wretches, if he will not let me in.'

'When you were allowed in, did you only ever see men from Marlborough?' Jane is pitifully eager for this surgeon to have tended others, maybe her brother. 'Were any from Cirencester?'

'I saw very few of any kind, before he stopped me entering the castle.'

'You do not remember their names?'

Mr Betterise looks at her sadly. 'My dear, I never knew names. The sick were too far gone to tell me.'

Chapter 9

A Plea to the King

More than forty rebel prisoners remain in Bridewell prison, up to the ankles in their own piss and shit. Martin Watts is there, still alive but suffering badly. Pressed up against his comrades, unable to move, he must stand in that foul place, in the dark, day and night.

Sometimes he wants to die and end it. But he hangs on grimly. He will not allow Marshal Smith the joy of killing him.

When they have been in the dungeon for two weeks, they begin to hope for change. Somehow they have written and smuggled out a petition to the King in Oxford and a letter to Parliament in London. Their treatment by Smith is now known in the outside world. Parliament orders their letter to be printed. The misery at Oxford Castle can no longer be ignored by the royalist high command.

This is the age of political writing. When Parliament first took a stand against the King's high-handed ways, censorship was stopped. At first, no one saw how important that would be. There is no way back. Words are the chief weapon in the civil war. All kinds of people are writing and publishing. Anyone can rush into print and cry out their thoughts. Other people are eager to read what they say.

One person who has suffered for his writing is John Lilburne, now held with the officers at Oxford Castle. He will become one of England's most famous radicals.

Another is called Edmund Chillenden. He too will become a champion of liberty – he will be a founding member of the Levellers, a fierce radical group. His time in Bridewell will help shape his views and make him ready to defy tyranny even at the risk of his life. What life is there, anyway, for the men buried alive in this foul dungeon?

So details of their plight become public. The passionate plea for an end to their abuse is probably the work of Chillenden. He dares not own up to it, for fear of Marshal Smith. Smith suspects him, though, and tries hard to prove that he wrote the letter.

When the dire list of Smith's tortures reaches the King, an order is given for an enquiry into the truth of the document. Six prisoners from

Bridewell are sent for. Chillenden is among them.

Martin is not. He has to wait in the hell-hole at Bridewell, praying that the six men will be believed. By now he knows better than to hope.

****

After what feels like an endless wait, the six men who went to give evidence return and are shoved back down into the dungeon. The guards' jeers tell what has happened. No one in the King's court will take any notice. The King himself will ignore their plight. There will be no let-up in their torture. Smith has got away with it.

Martin manages to squeeze himself through the rest and come nearer to Edmund Chillenden, so he hears the story. Squashed close together in the dark, their voices are low and intent.

'We six were put in irons and taken through the streets like criminals. We came to the headquarters of Sir Jacob Astley, the King's general. We did not see Astley, but were met by a man called Doctor Reeves who, we learned, is the King's Advocate. There were two others with him. They did not question us. Instead, they lectured us, telling us to take the old oath – to change sides, and fight in the King's army.'

'What said you to that?'

'We answered the same as always – that we had taken an oath already, which is to the King and Parliament. This we will maintain to the last drop of our blood. As for that oath they wanted us to take, we said we did not know whose it was, nor what was its authority. But we do know that the laws of the land provide that no oath may be forced upon us. We need swear no oath that does not have consent in Parliament.'

Another of the six spokesmen chimes in: 'We said these laws are our inheritance, which we shall defend and maintain as our true rights and liberties. In no way shall we betray them.'

Edmund Chillenden takes up the tale again. As Martin hugs his thin arms around himself and listens, he thinks Chillenden's next words sound clever. 'We begged to be excused from taking the oath they asked for, because we must not swear a solemn oath when its issues are in doubt for us – only when we are certain about the matter.'

Martin Watts reacts with a little smile. This answer is designed to defy and offend the enemy. Although the clever speech will do no good to the prisoners in this dungeon, he wants to cheer. It feels good simply to have someone stand up for them. 'So what did they say to that?'

'Smith cried out, *"Hark, hark, they are a-preaching!"*'

'And you preached on?'

'We did. We complained of our ill-treatment. We told them this was the way to kill us through starvation. We said that many are sick in this dungeon – we begged them to remove the sick, to some better place where they may have more air. Finally we said we hoped it was not the King's will, nor the pleasure of his council of war, thus to destroy us.'

Martin feels his heart quicken, though he is so starved and weak that it happens for no reason sometimes. 'And was there any response?'

Chillenden sounds weary. 'Doctor Reeves told us that it *is* the King's will and it *is* the pleasure of his war council to destroy us.' So Chillenden concludes in a drab tone: 'Then the doctor put on his spectacles and glared down his nose at us. He said we looked as fat as rabbits – and we were sent back again to this dungeon.'

Chapter 10

'We Shall All Die . . .'

The state of the men in the dungeon grows worse. The sick become weaker and weaker. One man is so ill that he helplessly has to relieve himself where he is, covering himself with his own waste. Another is troubled by continual vomiting. Nobody clears up after them. The stench is overwhelming. For the rest it is horrible to be so near these poor men.

One day Marshal Smith comes to the dungeon. The prisoners complain to him, begging again for the sick to be taken where there is more air. 'Let them be more comfortable and have better food, let people come to their aid. If nothing is done for them, they will not live long.'

Smith sticks to his usual story – that if they take the oath to serve the King, they may have anything they want. 'If you will not swear, then if you all die, I will not care. It is by your own choice and you will be your own murderers!'

He refuses to increase their rations. They may not have their shirts washed, so they are increasingly louse-ridden, which leads to more disease. He will not allow any friend to visit them, nor even their wives. He has been annoyed by complaints being printed and made public. Under a threat of an inspection, at last he is giving kinder treatment to the officers and gentlemen back at the castle. But these common men in the dungeon are at his mercy. Their leaders have been mocked by Doctor Reeves, the King's Advocate. Smith can punish and deprive them as he likes.

The prisoners are not the only people to suffer. Smith's cruelty is never rational. The man in charge of Bridewell – a civilian, not a soldier – is arrested by Smith for having a pot of food boiling over the fire for his own dinner. This unlucky jailer is dragged to the castle and imprisoned there, while Smith's own men eat his stew.

A prisoner called Giles Carter dies in great agony. Another called Caleb Rolfe also passes away.

****

When Giles Carter dies in the dungeon, the

other prisoners think about themselves. If they remain here, they will die one by one.

Martin Watts feels greatly affected by Giles Carter's death. He has been standing close to the sick man and wished he could help him. 'We shall perish. If we do nothing, we shall all die. If we want to live, we must take our fate into our own hands.'

The men talk together in dull voices. They sound as if they have given up hope – but they are not willing to endure Smith's abuse any longer. They are looking for a way out. Now, they are ready to try anything.

They have been locked up together long enough to have bonded. They can work together – and they will. They share one intent. They can stay here and die – or do something about it. They are all in agreement. The prisoners in Bridewell decide to escape.

Chapter 11

The Plan of Escape

In Bridewell, the prisoners are busy. People do escape. Doctor Calyton, a doctor of divinity, tries to escape from his misery at the castle, over a wall. He falls and fatally breaks his neck. Others who escape are recaptured by Smith, and badly punished. Even if they break out of their dungeon, the prisoners will be in a walled town guarded by soldiers. Somehow they will have to escape from Oxford itself, on foot, and knowing the alarm will soon be raised.

This is dispiriting. Still, these men are in despair already. Nothing now will put them off. They begin to dig a way out.

****

Since their jailers take no interest in them, it is easy to work unnoticed. First, they locate an outside wall. In some ways, their treatment has been oddly casual. Although many have been robbed of shoes and coats, others have been allowed to keep pocket knives. They would use these for eating – were they given any food. It is a strange aspect of war at this time, that nobody seems afraid that such prisoners will rush their guards or attack them.

They use their knives to tackle the wall. They also have a hook that is meant to hold a door open, which they have prised free to use. There is only room for one or two men to be digging at once. Making a tunnel is maddeningly slow. Scraping away at the mortar between building stones, they make grooves, then press in deeper. The mortar and rubble are carried to far corners of the dungeon and spread in the stinking wash of human filth on the floor.

Using such small tools for a heavy job seems as delicate as watchmaking. Sometimes the amounts they remove are little more than thimblefuls. Then suddenly a larger amount of stones will tumble free. Nobody can work for long. They are so weak they can only manage very short stints. They have to be quiet. All the time a watchman listens out for guards. At any approach they have to stop.

Martin Watts takes his turn. He is feeling ill. His stomach has turned to water and he fears he will not be able to make a run for freedom, even if they manage to get out. Still, he keeps going and digs when he can. The need to escape from this misery drives him hard. He finds strength he never knew he had. He learns how much determination he has in him. He uses a bookbinding knife that he somehow kept with him in a pocket, until the fine tool breaks. Then he is given the stronger iron door hook.

Martin works until he drops. Then someone else takes over.

He feels ill, but others are worse. He overhears whispering about what can be done for the weakest. Not much. It will be impossible to carry the sick. No one has the strength. They have to go on foot and must move fast. They have to swim the river.

One young man, who is desperately sick, weeps. The sound is heart-rending. He wants so badly to escape but, when he tries to help, he collapses at once. Gently the others remove him. Nobody knows this youth very well. Most of them are from Marlborough or Banbury. He is one of the prisoners captured at Cirencester.

Martin asks why the boy was not sent home with the rest of the troops from there. Nobody can say. 'What is his name?' No one knows that either. When Martin is resting from digging, he wants to go and ask, but he finds he is too feeble to struggle over to the sick boy.

****

It takes days. But they make a hole through the wall a yard deep. Finally they break through to the outside.

This is it.

****

Forty prisoners squeeze through the dungeon wall, into the fresh air. Six are too ill to move, and have to stay behind.

Martin Watts is one of the forty who escape. But soon he is feeling so weak he cannot keep up with the others as they flee. By the time they swim the river, Martin has lagged too far behind and has been left alone in a dark street. He is free, but helpless.

He keeps vomiting from whatever sickness he caught in prison. He finds his way somehow to a garden near the base of the castle. It is a poor hiding place; he knows he is doomed. He sinks down on the hard ground, with all hope draining from him. He is trapped in Oxford. It cannot be long before Marshal Smith and his men find him.

The disappointment is tragic, as Martin waits to be discovered.

Chapter 12

News – But None for Jane

At Saint George's Tower, the letter taken to Parliament, the one written by Edmund Chillenden, has had some results.

Marshal Smith is more nervous than he first appeared, but he brazens it out. When Parliament sends a hundred pounds to provide the prisoners with food, Smith makes this an excuse to stop spending the King's money.

This is a religious age. In fact, religion is one of the reasons they are fighting. Questions have been asked about the prisoners not being allowed to attend worship, even though the castle has a chapel. So Smith brings in a priest – though his sermons are crude rants against Parliament. When this priest asks for his fee, Smith claps him in irons, until the man is glad to leave without payment. He will not be back.

When Jane and other women visit the castle they continue to hear dreadful stories. They know Smith steals from prisoners, beats them, punishes them by burning them with lit match cord and by loading them with chains. He still provides little food and often no water. He keeps people in jail even after the King has formally pardoned them. He even recaptures men who have been freed, returns them to prison and then demands even more money to release them again. Some cannot pay a second ransom and die in prison.

Agents come to Oxford from Parliament to inspect conditions. The King permits this, so he can maintain that the letter of complaint was untrue. By now Marshal Smith has perfected a lie to excuse his actions. He claims that any men he has punished were stirring up mutiny. He often accuses his prisoners of plotting. Many of those he has treated worst cannot complain because they have died.

Smith tries to fool the agents. He lightens the harsh regime under which he holds the officers and gentlemen. The agents from Parliament will look most keenly into how he treats these captives – men of their own rank.

Smith now allows the captains and gentlemen to walk in the castle gardens, taking air and exercise. At last he even permits visits by their worried friends and careworn wives. So Captain Wingate's wife finally learns directly from her husband the full story of his appalling life in jail. She already knew he was kept in solitary confinement. She had herself made a complaint to Parliament, saying that he was denied books and writing tools, nearly starved and, on some days, not even given bread and water.

Now she hears things that are far worse. When the shocked Mrs Wingate leaves the castle after seeing the captain, Jane finds her almost speechless.

Mrs Wingate fixes her grief on a matter of money as she begins to share her trouble with Jane. 'Marshal Smith had a bill of exchange from my husband and Captain Austen for thirty pounds. Thirty pounds, Jane! That would have bought them many comforts – but he has never given them the money. We think he has stolen it for himself. When Captain Austen asked for it, Smith called Austen a shitty apprentice boy, and threatened to put him in chains, neck and heels, which is a very harsh punishment. Marshal Smith refused to allow my husband a Bible, and nor was he allowed to walk in the garden for his health, although he is not well. And Smith took away the mattress from his bed, so he must sleep only on the mattress cords . . .'

Mrs Wingate goes deathly quiet. Jane can see that her friend is distressed for worse reasons. She quietly presses her. Mrs Wingate can hardly bear to say what she has heard: 'Ah Jane, this is barbarous. A man was hanged – a criminal. Captain Wingate had been kept locked up alone until then. But Master Harfield, a minister from Banbury, was suddenly put in with my husband. The minister was kept in irons. Then—' She nearly gags. 'After the hanged man's corpse was cut down, it was thrown into the same room with them.'

'Oh no!'

'And left to rot.'

'Oh surely not!'

'This is true. I never heard such an unchristian thing.'

'How long did this continue?'

'Smith would not allow the body to be taken out for days. They were kept together all three – my ailing husband, the minister in chains, and the decomposing corpse.' Mrs Wingate is in tears. 'Smith does this on purpose, Jane. He will not let those who die be taken away until their corpses stink like poison. In this way he forces the prisoners to find money for their funerals.'

Jane tries to soothe the stricken woman, but Mrs Wingate has completely broken down. Jane takes her home.

****

In the next days, Jane spends much time trying to comfort Mrs Wingate. It helps take her own mind away from the futile search to learn her brother's fate. But giving comfort, where really there is none, is tiring. It wears down her spirit.

Like so many wives of men fighting in the civil war, Mrs Wingate has become a brave woman. She recovers, because she has to. It is her role to keep strong for her family. On the rare occasions when she can see her husband, she must present a brave face so she does not add to his anxiety.

Jane pleads with her to ask Captain Wingate if he knows anything about Nat. Mrs Wingate promises to ask. Indeed she does so. But she tells Jane her husband has heard nothing.

Jane feels an odd sense of unease. Since she trusts Mrs Wingate, she lets it pass.

****

When Parliament's agents leave Oxford, Marshal Smith soon stops letting friends and wives see the officers.

Mrs Wingate decides to travel to visit her young children, who have been left at home. She needs the comfort that seeing them will bring. While she is away, Jane may stay in her room, which is better than where Jane has been lodging.

Left quietly on her own, it is Jane's turn to fall victim to despair. She continues to visit the castle, still asking for news of her brother. Her pleas feel more hopeless than ever. Now the guards seem to know that her protector has gone away. Their manners become coarser, their words vile, their advances unbearable.

All the soldiers are jumpy. A rumour, which the troops will not confirm, suggests that prisoners from Bridewell have escaped. Smith is out looking for them.

****

In a battered mood, Jane takes herself away from the castle, walking. Nearby there is an ancient garden, called the Paradise. She knows the place. It is an old orchard, in the grounds of a medieval monastery. There, even so close to the scene of cruelty at Saint George's Tower, she knows she will find peace and fresh air, amid the innocent sounds of birdsong.

She has been to this garden before, seeking comfort. Few people ever come. So she is surprised to see someone here.

Barely aware of his surroundings, the man has collapsed. He looks half dead, from want and misery. Seeing Jane, he tries to struggle upright. He ends up only on his knees, in the act of vomiting. His stomach is too empty.

He looks like a vagrant. The gaunt, pale-faced figure has a wild beard and hair, and dry, staring eyes. Even from a distance his stench makes Jane recoil. It is Martin Watts.

Jane is terrified at first. Even so, she believes this is not a normal homeless man. She guesses that he is an escaped prisoner. She sees that he is more afraid than she is – afraid she may report him to the soldiers. Jane knows what going back to prison would mean to him, and his despair affects her deeply.

Jane looks around to see if they are watched.

'You escaped from Bridewell,' she says, certain this is true. She speaks in a low, careful tone, as if calming a stray dog. The man closes his eyes and slumps, thinking she is going to call out for help. But Jane Afton has an urgent need to speak to anyone who has been inside Marshal Smith's prison. 'I shall not betray you. Stand up if you can,' she orders him. She will not go and touch him. She is not that brave. 'For your own sake, you must come away from here.'

So Jane Afton leaves the Paradise garden, and Martin Watts finds the strength to follow. Jane, who was always the sensible one in her family, has reached her decision. She takes a strange man home with her.

Chapter 13

Martin's Life in Jane's Hands

First she gives him water.

Jane stands Martin in the yard by the pump and lets him gulp from a bowl as much as he wants. Almost at once he starts to know where he is again. Before Jane brings him into the house it is urgent to wash him. As he half strips, shyly, she commands, 'All off!' When he blushes, she adds, 'I have a brother. I have seen it before.'

Jane leaves him to it while she goes to her own lodgings to fetch the clothes she brought to Oxford for Nat. All the foul rags Martin has been wearing in prison will have to be burned. Even his shoes. Especially his shoes, in which he has stood for weeks in human waste.

At this time of day, luckily no one is at home. None of the other tenants who rent rooms where Mrs Wingate lives see Martin being stripped, scrubbed and dressed in a shirt. Jane brings him secretly indoors and warms him by the kitchen fire. Then she puts him in Mrs Wingate's bed. By this time, he has run out of strength. He lies there, barely conscious. Jane risks leaving him again and hurries to get help.

She goes for the surgeon, Mr Betterise. When she tells him her mission, the surgeon seems uneasy because he has suffered at Marshal Smith's hands himself – yet Jane persists. He sets aside his fear and comes with her to the house.

He exclaims over Martin's starved body. As he examines the poor man, he tells Jane to bring warm broth. 'A little only. His stomach is so unused to food, it may throw the first back up. You must feed him sips from a spoon. He has no wounds – that's one comfort.'

Martin stirred anxiously when the doctor arrived. He lets himself be examined, but seems relieved when it is over. He trembles violently. Jane brings another blanket. All this time he has not said one word.

'Can he speak?' asks Jane. 'Is he mute?'

'He has lost his trust.' Mr Betterise gazes at her. 'You will bring him back to the world with kindness. I have no doubt of it.'

Before the surgeon leaves, he cuts off Martin's matted hair and beard, throwing them in the kitchen fire. He does not need to explain. Jane has seen for herself that Martin is infested with lice. She senses that he was once clean and healthy. His current state shames him.

She feeds him. He vomits. She pauses, then feeds him again. She spoons in broth as she has done in the past when her brother was a sick child.

While Martin rests, worn out, Jane folds her hands modestly. She is frank about her nervousness of being alone with a strange man: 'I am a single woman. I have no husband to protect me. I must rely on you, sir, not to offend against my modesty.'

For the first time, Martin visibly revives. He indicates how helpless he is. Then he shakes his head ruefully, laughing until Jane has to laugh with him. She feels her fear subside.

He says his name. She tells him hers.

Jane leaves him to rest, but Martin cannot sleep. He lies on his back, watching a very small spider creep across the ceiling. He lets himself relax, enjoying the luxury of being in a bed for the first time in three months, with his skin newly clean, with good broth inside him. He turns his face against the smooth pillowcase. In the silence of this almost empty house, he considers how he came to be here, wonders what will happen to him now. There is nothing he can do about anything, and he no longer minds that.

Jane looks in, sees him still awake. She comes to his bedside, gives him more water, then states her request.

'I have a young brother. Nat is his name. A prisoner of Marshal Smith. He was taken at Cirencester, but he never came home with the rest and I can hear no news of him. Nat Afton. You are in his shirt.'

Martin looks down. That he is wearing Nat's shirt affects him painfully.

He knows he has probably seen Jane's beloved brother in the Bridewell dungeon. Nat is probably the boy they had to leave behind, too weak to move, too sick to escape – and if he is not helped soon, almost certainly dying.

Martin cannot bear to say this to the young woman who has saved him from his own plight. He takes the coward's way out. He tells Jane what is strictly true: that in prison he never heard the name Nat Afton.

He regrets it at once. He can see she believes he is lying.

Chapter 14

What Happened to Nat

It is indeed Nat who was left behind in the dungeon.

Nat Afton has had unexpected adventures. After being captured by Prince Rupert's men at Cirencester, instead of keeping out of trouble, as he always did before, he found himself in the worst trouble of his life.

He and his comrades were brought to Oxford in February. That was around a month ago.

Being starved, and whipped along the road on a four-day journey did not suit Nat at all. He has always wanted an easy time. But easy times are over for him now.

****

When they arrive, the prison in Oxford Castle is already full to bursting. Men from Marlborough and Banbury are taking all the space. Nat finds himself in an overflow group, which Marshal

Smith keeps locked up in local churches. Conditions there are better than in Saint George's Tower, and much better than in the filthy hole at Bridewell. Nat has no idea of that. He knows only that he is starving, parched and bitterly cold.

He is bored too. Marshal Smith does not allow exercise hours. And his staff have better things to do than supervise family visits. There is nothing to do, and no space to move anyway. Prisoners are crammed in, as many together as possible. They are forced to endure barbarous treatment that will, hopes Smith, soon kill them.

Nat is outraged when he works out that Smith plans to kill them by neglect. What has he done? He is an innocent. He joined up as a soldier, with little idea of what that meant. He did not care about the politics; he could as easily have joined the King's army, if they had asked him first.

Still, a strange loyalty comes over him now. He sticks with his choice. He does not know why Parliament is defying the King. But the men he was captured with, who do seem to know, are his mates and comrades. If they are rebels, he is one too.

At first they are made to work. Nat is angry about that. They are marched out daily to take up picks and spades, and help create the massive earth walls that protect the city for the King. Nat can dig but he does not like it. If he wanted to spend all day in the open, digging, he could have worked on a farm. At least he would then have had labourers' rations, instead of just a penny loaf and one pot of beer a day. It's not enough to keep a rat alive, let alone a rat who is being forced to build huge walls.

The life of a prisoner does not suit Nat at all – hardly surprising when no normal work suited him either. He has abandoned work of various kinds, to the sorrow of his dear relations, but he never even considered hard manual labour. He wants to go back to his life as a tavern tapster. It was a poor life, but Nat was comfortable with it.

A life like that may not be the kind of freedom that hot radicals are preaching. But it is Nat Afton's birthright. He even had a degree of choice. In prison, he begins to value this lost freedom. So, by taking that away, the King's jailer Marshal Smith has created yet another rebel. Nat is not merely angry. Light-headed from lack of food, he will easily fly into honest rage.

When the Cirencester prisoners are asked to swear the oath to the King, Nat refuses. He hates being told what to do. He feels betrayed by the other men, who change sides so easily.

Over a thousand of Nat's comrades do take

the oath. They differ from the Marlborough prisoners, who were so steadfast in refusing. Smith does not tell the men from Cirencester how the others reacted. They are left to make their own judgements – though they are told that their town has agreed to support King Charles. So they take the oath, and are duly sent home. A thousand fewer mouths to feed is a bonus, even at only one penny farthing a day.

Nat Afton is removed from the rest before they leave, and is accused of criminal acts. Nat has helped vandalise the church where they are held prisoner. In his current mood, he is all too ready to listen when others tell him this ornate house of God is an outrage. Many in Cirencester, where he and his companions come from, are puritans, who hate decorated churches like these high Anglican ones in Oxford. They want churches to be bare places, with basic services based on the Bible. Simplicity, they believe, is the way to pure religion.

Nat is influenced simply by the fact that this church is his jail. Locked in, with nothing to occupy their time but dismantling carved screens and smashing ancient stained glass, he and a few others do much damage. King Charles is forced to pay compensation to the church authorities.

When the King's men attempt to identify the culprits, Nat flies into a rage. He wants to go home. He knows he has lost his chance by refusing to swear the oath. He is starting to feel worried. Whereas most of the prisoners dully accept whatever is done to them, Nat Afton runs amuck. He comes out yelling. When asked if he did the damage, he replies yes he did and by God he would do it again. He curses everyone from the King down, then calls Provost Marshal Smith an evil son of a whore to his face.

This is not a good idea. But Nat has no education. He has not been taught to judge ideas or to express them with restraint.

Marshal Smith beats his own kind of education into Nat. He attacks him with a cane – the cane he leans on because of his lame leg. He beats Nat until blood runs all over him. Then Smith burns Nat's fingers to the bone with glowing match cord. This is the way soldiers on both sides make people own up to being spies. There is no point with Nat, who has confessed to damaging the church already. He has nothing more to tell them. The torture is pointless, carried out for the foul delight of bullies.

Nat is not sent back to the damaged church. He is thrown into the dungeon at Bridewell.

He stays there when most of his comrades are freed and leave Oxford. He is still there when forty other men are dumped inside, including Martin Watts. Nat's wounds have never been treated. They have festered and grown worse by the day. He is very sick.

But he does not believe his condition is serious. Cheery faith in the future has always been his way.

When the prisoners' escape plan goes into action, Nat tries to help dig, though he is no longer up to working. Even so, he is sure he will recover enough when the men make their run for it. Nat tells himself that if he can only escape from prison, he will reform. He will become a soldier in the cause of freedom. He will lead a good life, working hard. His family will be proud of him.

As Nat slowly has to face the fact that he will not be fit to escape, he weeps. His sobs are raw, though he is so dehydrated no tears flow.

Reality finally hits him. He sees that this is all there is for him. He must end his days in jail.

****

The forty men who are able to escape all go out through the wall. Six have to be left behind.

When Marshal Smith learns what has happened, he is furious. Since he cannot reach the men who escaped, he turns his rage on those who were too weak to go. The man lacks all logic.

Nat is now put in irons. He has chains weighing thirty pounds that tie his neck to his feet, so he cannot move. The pain is terrible. The misery increases as Smith now holds back bread from the six men, only supplying water.

Eventually Nat is taken from the dungeon. On Thursday or Friday – he has lost all track of time – he is taken to Saint George's Tower at the castle. His fetters are taken off. As the blood flows back to his stricken limbs, the pain feels even worse but he is too ill to scream. He is so ill he is in a kind of trance. Put into a room where there are about sixty other prisoners, he finds they are all sick with smallpox. The room stinks. It is cramped, noxious and unhealthy, though Nat bears it very quietly.

He knows he has come here to die.

Chapter 15

A Long Night of Freedom

Kind treatment is such a great luxury that Martin can barely enjoy it. This feels like a dream.

For nearly four months he has been either high in the tower or below ground in the dungeon. Now he is lying in a soft bed. Normal street sounds come to him through the leaded window. Since Oxford is a garrison town, there are plenty of noises even after curfew.

Jane has found wood, so a small fire glows in the grate, its flames lazily leaping when she places new sticks on it. She saves money, lighting neither candles nor rush-lights.

Jane has to sleep in this room. She has taken the truckle bed where Mrs Wingate's maid sleeps when they are here. Rolling on castors, it pulls out from under the main bed where Martin is. Jane guards her modesty. She stays fully dressed. In any case she has given the blanket to Martin. March nights are cold.

Jane cannot sleep either. She is wondering what she can do with this fugitive.

****

When the surgeon was here to attend Martin, he warned that tongues would wag. The people of Oxford are not all pleased to have the King and his men living among them, but those who do not support the royal cause keep quiet about it. Jane must assume everyone supports the King. That everyone here is against the prisoners; that everyone wants them back in jail, dying of neglect.

The forty men who escaped will have a hard time getting away. Even if they can filter through the royalist lines and swim the river, they must pass through hostile country. The nearest safe haven is Parliament's stronghold at Reading, at least twenty-five miles away.

How is Jane to take this man there?

****

He is awake. When he sees her eyes open too, he smiles a little in the dim firelight.

Martin is aware of Jane's great anxiety. Although she has full charge of him, he in turn considers her; he begins to think about how he may settle her fears. For the first time in his life, Martin Watts has a reason to give care to someone else. He is a good man and ready to do this.

Besides, he has been studying Jane Afton. He has never had close contact with women, nor has he even seen one during his months of captivity. He continues to gaze her way, liking what he sees.

Martin is man enough to bluff; he makes it seem that he is looking her way by chance. Even so, Jane knows what he is thinking.

****

Hours pass quietly. Outside the house, the streets finally grow still. It is the dead of night.

Jane comes to bring Martin water. His body has quickly healed and is nearly normal, yet he cannot drink enough. Sitting on the edge of the bed, she asks him about himself. Martin starts talking. He has not had a proper conversation since the fall of Marlborough. Stumbling at first, he tells of his childhood and schooling, then his work at John Hammond's bookshop. He speaks of books, and why they are important. He talks of how he hopes one day to sell books and news-sheets once again. By the time he falls silent, Jane almost knows more about Martin than he knows about himself.

In return, she tells him of her life. Although she speaks of her two sisters and their families, it is her brother Nat who takes first place. It seems like a ritual of mourning. Jane feels as if she is sharing vital memories of someone who has died – retelling a childhood before it is lost, to fix it for the empty future. She loved Nat, though he was a rascal. Stories about their early lives come rushing back to her, even stories she had forgotten.

This is a conversation Jane will have with no one else. Once she is done, only private grief remains. She has resigned herself. She knows she will never see Nat alive again.

Still, Jane wants to know his fate, to know for sure. The time has come for honesty. At last Martin feels able to tell her what he fears about the young man left in Bridewell. Jane describes Nat. Martin says nothing, but his silence gives an answer.

Jane weeps. Martin by instinct reaches to comfort her. She is cold. He pulls her under the covers alongside himself. So he holds her against his thin shoulder, while she grieves for her brother's suffering and her loss of him. Patiently Martin holds her in that chaste embrace until Jane is worn out and falls asleep. For a while longer Martin stays awake, taking his own comfort simply from the woman's warm presence in his arms. Then he too slumbers.

Chapter 16

Martin's Cruel Fate

He wakes first.

A soldier, trained to react fast, would be out of bed in an instant, pulling on his boots and his sword. Martin responds more slowly, but he can tell something has gone wrong. He has no weapons. He cannot defend himself.

Whatever noise woke him signals danger. He leaves the bed where Jane still sleeps. He puts on the britches, stockings and shoes that he knows she means to give to him. He finds himself stronger from being fed and rested, yet he is still shaky on his feet.

He can hear voices now. They are the wrong voices for normal life in a lodging house.

He makes his way quietly from the room. Terror of what is to happen to him makes his heart bump painfully. He can tell the house is being searched. Doors are being banged. He hears protests. A stranger here, he cannot find a safe place to hide. He stands no chance.

Somehow tongues have already wagged. Perhaps the burning of his clothes gave away that a prisoner was here. Perhaps somebody saw him, or saw Jane with the surgeon. How it happened does not matter. Marshal Smith's men are in the house.

Of course they find Martin. He has barely reached the downstairs, seeking a way out of the house. He is unable to resist.

As they are dragging him out of doors, Jane comes running in distress. A day ago she had never met this man. Now he has relied on her for help. He is her responsibility. She screams at the soldiers to leave him alone.

Jane knows that to be locked in that prison once was bad enough. For Martin Watts, to have to face returning to such an intolerable place must be unbearable. His look of despair is breaking her heart.

The look on her face breaks his own. Someone cares for his fate.

****

The soldiers have gained the wrong idea about these two. They allow Martin a strange courtesy of war. One says, 'Say farewell to your wife, wretch!' – and stands back to let him go to Jane.

Martin does not hesitate. 'Thanks,' he replies dryly. 'She thought I had run off with a dairy maid. It is a joy to her to know I am merely a guest, enjoying fine hospitality from Provost Marshal Smith.'

Talking about books with Jane last night has given something back to him: ideas and imagination. As Jane hears him joke, she knows he has renewed his courage. It was an empty shell she found collapsed yesterday in the garden, but she is seeing the real man now.

****

He winks. It is the first time in his life he has ever winked at a woman, but he carries it off bravely.

'Come, wife!' Martin smiles into her eyes, sharing the joke. For one shocked minute, Jane resists. Then her panic stills. He wraps Jane in his arms tenderly, as a married man really might on parting from his wife. Quickly he promises to find her brother if he can and to see what can be done for him. He thinks that is what Jane wants – and so she does, though another longing starts to affect her too.

The soldiers are not rushing them. For one thing, the brutes are enjoying the idea that

Martin Watts will die in prison, so these are the last ever moments together for the couple.

'I never had a wife,' murmurs Martin very privately to Jane, from close to. That answers the unasked question usefully, though it seems a strange moment for him to declare himself available. 'But if I did, I should not want anyone sweeter or kinder.'

It is his one chance in life to kiss a young woman, and he takes it. He takes it like a man who knows he may never have such a chance again. Jane Afton is a decent woman, but this poor fellow is about to lose everything, so she kisses him back, and does so most gladly – as he must be able to tell.

'Be brave,' she whispers urgently. 'Keep in good heart.'

****

Under one arm Jane is carrying a coat she brought to Oxford to give to Nat. When Martin releases her, she holds the coat open for him so he puts it on. The soldiers do not steal it, at least not while she is watching them.

But then they come and take Martin. Their brief period of courtesy to the prisoner is over. They are violent and rough with him. He is shoved and dragged along the street within a close knot of armed soldiers. Jane runs after, but is kept from him.

When they reach Saint George's Tower, as he is about to be pushed inside, Martin manages to shake off his guards for a moment. Jane sees him turn back. He knows she is there. She sees him raise an arm to her. Then he is hauled inside and lost to her. She knows that may be her last sight of this man for ever.

He has had a short glimpse of freedom but he has lost it. After all Martin has endured, it is the cruellest fate.

Chapter 17

Afterword

Of the forty men who went out through the wall, only four are recaptured. One of them is Martin Watts.

Martin is not put back into the black dungeon at Bridewell, which he knows would surely have killed him. Instead, he is returned to the room at Saint George's Tower where he was first imprisoned. It has grown even more foul. All the men there are sick. Among them, by asking and searching, he finds and identifies Nat Afton.

The boy is close to death, too sick by now even to know that Martin is there. He does not recognise his own coat, which Martin is wearing. Within a day, Jane's brother dies, but at least he has someone beside him, seeing him into his safe release from misery.

Martin hunches up in sorrow. He thrusts his hands deep into the pockets of Nat's coat, thinking of Jane. *Keep in good heart . . .* Her words console him as much as any line of scripture.

He is a different prisoner from the one who was here before. Give a man a goal and you give him hope. He has escaped once. Now he believes he has a reason to escape again. Now he believes it is possible. He will keep trying.

****

Some of the prisoners at Oxford do regain their liberty.

In May John Lilburne is exchanged for a royalist. He goes on to have a long life of campaigning for freedom, annoying all who are in authority.

In June, Captain Wingate and Edmund Chillenden escape. Chillenden will become a leading figure in the Leveller movement, arguing for the rights of all men to be equal. Wingate and Chillenden publish stories of the prisoners' terrible treatment in Oxford jail. Three hundred and fifty years later, their passionate words denouncing Provost Marshal Smith will still horrify readers.

John Franklin, the Member of Parliament for Marlborough, is less lucky. His son, John Franklin Junior, has already died in Saint George's Tower.

The father is subjected to deliberate cruelties. Cavalier prisoners, low men who have been arrested for low crimes, are put in the same room with him, where they carouse drunkenly all night. Franklin is a sick man. In July he dies without ever being freed.

Unknown numbers of nameless ordinary men perish in Oxford at the hands of Provost Marshal Smith. Yet in the end, there is such public outrage that Smith is brought to justice. Even the King can no longer pretend not to know what has happened in his name. Smith is removed. He is pilloried and punished.

Even so, the hard system of having to wait for ransom or a prisoner exchange means that more of Parliament's supporters will end their days in jail. Disease spreads quickly where many are penned together in poor conditions; it is even called jail fever. Only when the King is near defeat and Parliament's army captures Oxford – a whole three years later – will all the prisoners who survive be set free.

****

Long before that, Jane Afton has learned of her brother's death in prison. With Mrs Wingate's help – and after money is given to Smith – Jane manages to obtain Nat's body so she can give him a burial. There is nothing to keep her in Oxford, so she goes home.

She has no reason to expect further news of anyone she met on her sad trip. She returns to her old life in Cirencester. She lives alone still, unable to bear the reproach of her sisters, who seem to blame her for not saving Nat. They cannot believe what Jane tells them about the prison and the prisoners' dreadful suffering.

So Jane keeps to herself. She works. She rents the same tiny cottage. One up, one down. Smaller than many stables. She lives quietly. And perhaps sometimes, on a dark evening alone by the firelight, she remembers the man she tried to help, and lets herself wonder a little.

Until one day she wonders no longer. One day someone knocks on her door and she finds a gaunt, pale, shy man, with his body and soul scarred by suffering. He looks serious, though not gloomy. He looks pleased that somehow he has found her. She had told him where she lived and he remembered carefully. His arrival on her doorstep is not quite unexpected. Just as he believed he would escape again, Jane too had faith.

He tips his head on one side, wanting to see if he is welcome. Jane cannot help it, she bursts into tears.

'Come, wife,' says Martin Watts, reminding her of their last meeting, as he holds open his arms to comfort her. 'Keep in good heart!'

She is not his wife, but she will be. It is a fortune of war. And for them both, this at least is a gentle fate.

About the Author

Lindsey Davis is best known for her twenty volume mystery series about Roman detective Marcus Didius Falco, and her new series about his adopted daughter, Flavia Albia.

She has also written *Rebels and Traitors,* an epic novel set during the same time as *A Cruel Fate*.

If you enjoyed this book and would like to hear more from Lindsey Davis, email lindseydavisnews@hodder.co.uk and request to be added to her newsletter mailing list.

Books In The Series

Amy's Diary	Maureen Lee
Beyond the Bounty	Tony Parsons
Bloody Valentine	James Patterson
Blackout	Emily Barr
Chickenfeed	Minette Walters
Cleanskin	Val McDermid
The Cleverness of Ladies	Alexander McCall Smith
Clouded Vision	Linwood Barclay
A Cool Head	Ian Rankin
A Cruel Fate	Lindsey Davis
The Dare	John Boyne
Doctor Who: Code of the Krillitanes	Justin Richards
Doctor Who: Made of Steel	Terrance Dicks
Doctor Who: Magic of the Angels	Jacqueline Rayner
Doctor Who: Revenge of the Judoon	Terrance Dicks
Doctor Who: The Silurian Gift	Mike Tucker
Doctor Who: The Sontaran Games	Jacqueline Rayner
A Dreadful Murder	Minette Walters
A Dream Come True	Maureen Lee
The Escape	Lynda La Plante
Follow Me	Sheila O'Flanagan
Four Warned	Jeffrey Archer
Full House	Maeve Binchy
Get the Life You Really Want	James Caan
The Grey Man	Andy McNab
Hello Mum	Bernardine Evaristo
Hidden	Barbara Taylor Bradford

How to Change Your Life in 7 Steps	John Bird
Humble Pie	Gordon Ramsay
Jack and Jill	Lucy Cavendish
Kung Fu Trip	Benjamin Zephaniah
Last Night Another Soldier	Andy McNab
Life's New Hurdles	Colin Jackson
Life's Too Short	Val McDermid, Editor
Lily	Adèle Geras
The Little One	Lynda La Plante
Love is Blind	Kathy Lette
Men at Work	Mike Gayle
Money Magic	Alvin Hall
One Good Turn	Chris Ryan
The Perfect Holiday	Cathy Kelly
The Perfect Murder	Peter James
Quantum of Tweed: The Man with the Nissan Micra	Conn Iggulden
Raw Voices: True Stories of Hardship and Hope	Vanessa Feltz
Reading My Arse!	Ricky Tomlinson
Rules for Dating a Romantic Hero	Harriet Evans
A Sea Change	Veronica Henry
Star Sullivan	Maeve Binchy
Strangers on the 16:02	Priya Basil
Survive the Worst and Aim for the Best	Kerry Katona
The 10 Keys to Success	John Bird
Tackling Life	Charlie Oatway
Today Everything Changes	Andy McNab
Traitors of the Tower	Alison Weir
Trouble on the Heath	Terry Jones
Twenty Tales from the War Zone	John Simpson
We Won the Lottery	Danny Buckland
Wrong Time, Wrong Place	Simon Kernick

Lose yourself in a good book with Galaxy®

Curled up on the sofa,
Sunday morning in pyjamas,
just before bed,
in the bath or
on the way to work?

Wherever, whenever,
you can escape
with a good book!

So go on...
indulge yourself with
a good read and the
smooth taste of
Galaxy® chocolate.

Proudly supports Quick Reads

Read more at Galaxy Chocolate

Galaxy is a registered trademark. © Mars 2012

Quick Reads are brilliant short new books written by bestselling writers to help people discover the joys of reading for pleasure.

Find out more at **www.quickreads.org.uk**

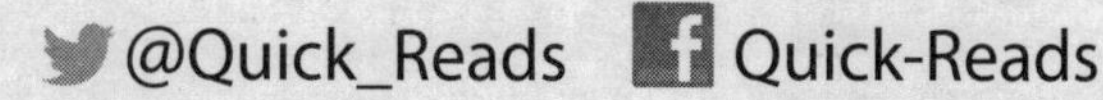
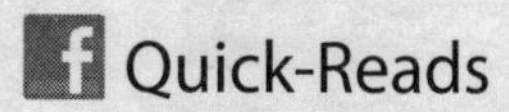

@Quick_Reads Quick-Reads

We would like to thank all our funders:

We would also like to thank all our partners in the Quick Reads project for their help and support: NIACE, unionlearn, National Book Tokens, The Reading Agency, National Literacy Trust, Welsh Books Council, The Big Plus Scotland, DELNI, NALA

At Quick Reads, World Book Day and World Book Night we want to encourage everyone in the UK and Ireland to read more and discover the joy of books.

World Book Day is on 6 March 2014
Find out more at **www.worldbookday.com**

World Book Night is on 23 April 2014
Find out more at **www.worldbooknight.org**

Hidden

Barbara Taylor Bradford

Drama, heartbreak and new beginnings.
This is a gripping story from a master storyteller.

On the surface, Claire Saunders has it all. She has a rewarding career in fashion and a talented concert pianist daughter. Her loving husband is one of the country's most trusted diplomats.

But every now and again, she has to plaster her face in heavy make-up and wears sunglasses. She thinks she's hidden her secret from her best friends, but they know her too well.

Can her friends get her out of harm's way and protect her from a man who is as ruthless as he is charming and powerful? And along the way, can Claire learn to stop protecting the wrong people?

Harper

Blackout

Emily Barr

You wake up in a strange room,
with no idea how you got there.

You are abroad, in a city you have never visited before.

You have no money, no passport, no phone.

And there is no sign of your baby.

What do you do?

Headline Review

Rules for Dating a Romantic Hero

Harriet Evans

Do you believe in happy endings?

Laura Foster used to be a hopeless romantic. She was obsessed with meeting her own Prince Charming until she grew up and realised real life doesn't work like that.

Then she met Nick. A romantic hero straight from a fairytale, with a grand country estate and a family tree to match.

They've been together four years now and Laura can't imagine ever loving anyone the way she loves Nick.

Now, though, Nick is keeping secrets from Laura. She's starting to feel she might not be 'good enough' for his family.

Can an ordinary girl like Laura make it work with one of the most eligible men in the country?

Harper

Four Warned

Jeffrey Archer

These four short stories from a master storyteller are packed full of twists and turns.

In Stuck on You, Jeremy steals the perfect ring for his fiancée.

Albert celebrates his 100th birthday, and is pleased to be sent The Queen's Birthday Telegram. Why hasn't his wife received hers?

In Russia, businessman Richard plots to murder his wife. He thinks he's found the answer when his hotel warns him: Don't Drink the Water.

Terrified for her life, Diana will do whatever it takes to stick to the warning given to drivers: Never Stop on the Motorway …

Every reader will have their favourite story – some will make you laugh, others will bring you to tears. And every one of them will keep you spellbound.

Pan Books

A Cruel Fate

Lindsey Davis

As long as war exists, this story will matter.

Martin Watts, a bookseller, is captured by the king's men. Jane Afton's brother Nat is taken too. They both suffer horrible treatment as prisoners-of-war.

In Oxford Castle jailer William Smith tortures, beats, starves and deprives his helpless victims. Can Jane rescue her sick brother before he dies of neglect? Will Martin dare to escape?

Based on real events in the English Civil War, Lindsey Davis retells the grim tale of Captain Smith's abuse of power in Oxford prison – where many died in misery though a lucky few survived.

Hodder and Stoughton

The Escape

Lynda La Plante

Is a change of identity all it takes to leave prison?

Colin Burrows is desperate. Recently sent to prison for burglary, he knows that his four-year sentence means he will miss the birth of his first child.

Sharing a cell with Colin is Barry Marsden. Barry likes prison life. He has come from a difficult family and been in and out of foster homes all his life. In prison, he has three meals a day and has discovered a talent for drawing. He doesn't want to leave.

Sad to see his cellmate looking depressed, Barry hatches a plan to get Colin out of jail for the birth. It's a plan so crazy that it might just work.

Bestselling author Lynda La Plante's exciting tale of one man's escape from jail is based on a true story.

Simon & Schuster

Why not start a reading group?

If you have enjoyed this book, why not share your next Quick Read with friends, colleagues, or neighbours.

A reading group is a great way to get the most out of a book and is easy to arrange. All you need is a group of people, a place to meet and a date and time that works for everyone.

Use the first meeting to decide which book to read first and how the group will operate. Conversation doesn't have to stick rigidly to the book. Here are some suggested themes for discussions:

- How important was the plot?
- What messages are in the book?
- Discuss the characters – were they believable and could you relate to them?
- How important was the setting to the story?
- Are the themes timeless?
- Personal reactions – what did you like or not like about the book?

There is a free toolkit with lots of ideas to help you run a Quick Reads reading group at **www.quickreads.org.uk**

Share your experiences of your group on Twitter @Quick_Reads

For more ideas, offers and groups to join visit Reading Groups for Everyone at **www.readingagency.org.uk/readinggroups**

Enjoy this book?

Find out about all the others at **www.quickreads.org.uk**

For Quick Reads audio clips as well as videos and ideas to help you enjoy reading visit the BBC's Skillswise website **www.bbc.co.uk/quickreads**

Skillswise

Join the Reading Agency's Six Book Challenge at **www.readingagency.org.uk/sixbookchallenge**

THE READING AGENCY

Find more books for new readers at
www.newisland.ie
www.barringtonstoke.co.uk

Free courses to develop your skills are available in your local area. To find out more phone 0800 100 900.

For more information on developing your skills in Scotland visit **www.thebigplus.com**

Want to read more? Join your local library. You can borrow books for free and take part in inspiring reading activities.